Each Path a Red Thread

Briane Willis

Each Path a Red Thread

Briane Willis

www.BrianeWillis.com

Cover art by Cristina Pongetti

Cover design by Chani Taylor

ISBN-13: 979-8-9875920-4-5

To the AO3 community
who made it possible.

Prologue

The Labyrinth coiled around the very heart of Crete.

Bounded by lapping mazarine waters, and clustered with low bushy trees against the ochre soil, it was a place of stark opposites. The maze was most dramatic of all; a shadowed engraving on the landscape, holding a darker truth.

People spoke of the Labyrinth's grandeur. Even Princess Ariadne—in her removed perch in the palace on the hill—heard the tales. Such cleverness, they said of her father's design, no one would discover its pattern. Such ingenuity.

She learned to ignore the accolades and mindless exultation.

Despite how flippantly the king treated the residents of Knossos, they lauded him for his containment of the Minotaur within those barren walls. Everyone feared the beast more than they needed a benevolent leader, it would seem. This she found incomprehensible. Fear made the people weak and pliable, and most effective in stoking terror was a mysterious other, foreign and labeled dangerous. This was a far simpler choice than fearing the ones with true authority.

Few people realized monsters take different shapes. What one individual may consider evil, another may deem righteous. Ariadne swallowed this understanding like a cold stone.

The gods manipulated all. The king ruled his subjects. And everyone adopted this hierarchy without protest. Save for Ariadne.

She often imagined tossing her father inside the Labyrinth.

Let him try to outwit the gods, persevere over nature, and conquer the maze.

But the exercise was unsatisfying.

King Minos had expected his firstborn to be a son. Thereafter, Ariadne continued this unintended pattern of disappointing him; she cried too much as a baby, didn't grow fast enough, couldn't argue intelligently enough.

For many years, she worked relentlessly to earn his respect and acceptance. It was for naught.

She had still been a child when his harsh words had ripped into her, a cataclysm of vocal cords and sentiments that left her reeling.

"You are pathetic, girl. Fragile and sentimental. You are a worse outcome than not having a child at all. You should never have been born."

Her father's voice was icy while her mother uttered not a word.

Ariadne ran from the palace then, stifling her tears, pushing them down until she thought she would burst. Before fleeing, she placed into a canvas bag a golden mirror from the queen, the dagger she had stolen from the armory, and a flask of water.

Night had clustered close and she cursed herself for forgetting a light. The crowded tension in her chest tightened. She hadn't ventured into the city alone before. She didn't know where to go.

As she rushed through the empty streets, a tall form overtook her, and she stumbled into a fall. The nearby wall of the Labyrinth reached skyward, and cut the southern wind, leaving the air stale and fraught. Ariadne gasped as moonlight glinted on the attacker's knife. The shape before her hunched and crept nearer.

"Give me everything you've got in that bag, girl…"

"I have nothing," she said, crawling away.

"Ah, I doubt that. I know the princess when I see her."

Ariadne fumbled for her dagger, but the thief was quicker. She screamed, a piercing sound launched into the relative calm of the slumbering streets. Silence followed. The thief cupped a hand to his ear in a mocking gesture, and chuckled.

Then, a formless roar erupted.

From the Labyrinth sprang a voice, scalding as molten metal. It lashed out at such a volume the ground shook. Ariadne's tears fell swiftly, her mouth hanging open as she stiffened on the ground. The thief froze, his knife held high, suspended. He quaked as another roar cascaded over them. The bellow seemed to originate in too high a place, perhaps atop the Labyrinth wall itself. Stricken, the thief clutched his ragged cloak about him and darted eastward, snatching glances over his shoulder.

Ariadne remained unmoving in a heap, chest heaving and cheeks wet. To her astonishment, she accepted her death in the sudden stillness. Whoever frightened the thief boasted power beyond what she could ever hope to possess.

But her savior didn't appear. The individual stayed out of sight and silent.

Soon, her breath leveled. She collected her bag and said, "Thank you. You saved me. That was very kind."

There was no audible reply.

Dejected, she returned to the palace before anyone knew she was missing.

Years later, having weighed the possibilities, Ariadne concluded the voice had belonged to the Minotaur. The realization came to her in a dream, a certainty buried in the valleys of her mind, roots sent deep into her very being.

And so she set out to help him, a repayment for saving her young life.

Ariadne found herself thinking of him throughout each day. During her own studies, she considered his lack of opportunities to learn. While she drafted ways to improve Knossos's crop rotation, a task she imagined fit for the son of a king, she worried the Minotaur didn't have sufficient food.

The memory of their first encounter stood like recently burned flesh, bright and raw. She began listening to the stories from the city with deepened fervor. She asked her mother countless questions about the beast in the Labyrinth. He became her only friend, that creature who had answered her plea and sent her would-be attacker running. She coveted his strength.

Stranger still, she identified a surprising seed of envy toward the Minotaur. He was a prisoner, but he owed nothing to anyone, had no responsibilities, and lived to destroy. To consider such might sent a thrill through her, rapid and hungry. If she was honest with herself, she could almost understand why the gods did what they did.

Ariadne also resented his circumstance. The people banished the Minotaur for no crime he had committed; he was simply created and punished. But she would correct this wrong. He deserved more than the world had given him.

His creators left him to suffer, yet they could not forget him. He demanded their attention with his ground-shaking calls each night. Ariadne believed these calls were acts of defiance and she relished his outpouring, a single option for proclaiming his discontent.

But even stars fade when clouds roll in, leaving hazy skies and a chill in their wake. So too did the Minotaur's roars begin to fade, as if finally succumbing to a sullen sorrow.

Chapter 1

Princess Ariadne flicked at a morsel with her fork, ignoring a simmering headache. King Minos and Queen Aika sat on either side of her and no one spoke. Her father read various papers, his dinner untouched. Her mother worked patiently through each bite, cutting the perfectly browned meat into sections appropriate for a queen to chew.

Ariadne was on the verge of excusing herself when a noise rose, distant but hair-raising. They all paused, familiar with the cry, but Minos was the first to resume reading. Aika glanced at Ariadne, her right shoulder lifting gracefully, as if to say, "the beast still lives. "

Ariadne looked away, fists balling in her lap. They feigned disinterest when the Minotaur was the only fascinating subject on the entire island. His bellows came less often of late, and she had a distinct worry there was a reason.

She chewed another mouthful despite her full stomach, too distracted to taste the tender meat.

The Minotaur's call had a tendency to burst from the Labyrinth at unexpected moments; during a ceremony, to interrupt the birth of a child, or as people broke bread. Across the city his vocalizations swept, the thunder of its force sending shivers down the backs of children and adults alike. The sound reverberated within form and flesh, forcing each person to consider the creature capable of such a noise.

Ariadne experienced a different reaction. Dread did not twist in her belly, nor did she tremble. When her thoughts dwelt on him, no rope of terror tightened her throat. Most frequently, she thought of him and noted his potential. She rarely considered her resulting jealousy, choosing to shove such a feeling out of sight.

"I wish to leave the table and return to my studies," she said.

"Certainly, dear." Queen Aika appraised her. "At the late hour, perhaps you should sleep. You're looking tired."

Ariadne placed her utensils on the platter and rose. "Yes, Mother. Goodnight."

Minos didn't acknowledge Ariadne's departure. She left the room and her parents resumed their silent, strained routine.

Ariadne contemplated the beast often, trapped inside a prison more constricting than her own. She imagined him walking the narrow paths of the Labyrinth in an endless cycle of isolation and confinement, consoled solely by the drifting stars above. The Minotaur had nothing to observe beyond the changing sky through dawn and dusk.

How the stars must shift over the tedious, dreary days.

Sometimes, Ariadne tried to visualize how he might gaze at the constellations, seeking understanding, context, perhaps companions among the points of light. Anything to combat the shadowed emptiness of a maze, designed to keep its victims within its imposing walls. Countless victims, all lost, all doomed to a future not of their making. Like her.

She refused to accept this, for the Minotaur or herself.

The layers of her pearlescent dress fluttered as she walked the palace hallways to her room, nestled at the end of the eastern wing. A guard was stationed nearby, and she inclined her head at him. His only recognition of her presence was a slight incline of his chin.

What a terrible job, standing here, guarding me from the world. If only he knew how he should guard the world from me.

The guard knew the reasons for his duty. The Minotaur likely had no conception of why his days were monotonous. In her estimation, that was the worst part.

Born and banished, never to know one's own origins, let alone direct one's future. This will change.

She clicked her door shut and went to her preferred seat. The windowsill was plush with cushions, a blanket, books, and blank parchment. She shoved off her shoes and gazed at the Labyrinth.

Night made the maze appear bottomless. The Minotaur's punishment was simply another way for the gods to torment lesser beings, she knew. The gods were despicable. They subjugated, exploited, and violated with no regard for the consequences, demanding adoration and worship above all. Ariadne loathed their hypocrisies, their self-absorption.

She summoned her wrath and spat out her window.

Of course, she did not dare even whisper her most private disdain toward the gods. Not yet. She must hold her disgust in secret, feeding and encouraging it to grow. This was a straightforward task, and a satisfying one. Ariadne excelled at being patient.

A slight breeze from the window ruffled her skirt, and she tugged the blanket over her arms. There was an irony to her disdain, she knew. She was the granddaughter of Helios, the god of the sun. At her most generous, she could acknowledge that this connection wasn't wholly detestable, for at least Helios didn't intrude on the lives of people.

But he does not dictate who I am or what I do. These are choices I make and through this control, I claim true freedom.

The guards at the palace gate rotated at the end of their shift. She watched them fulfill their functions, wordlessly and in precisely the same manner. She was much the same, existing however and wherever King Minos directed.

Fate was the enemy. Fate had brought her here to the palace, born to parents who would never accept her. And she would be free of its claws, even if she had to break each curved, pointed nail herself.

***

In the dreams that descended that night, she returned to the night the thief found her. His voice rasped and his feet shuffled. There was menace on his breath and in his hunched shoulders. And then the Minotaur heard her call and responded, securing her survival, and her gratitude.

She had lost control of her life then. The Minotaur had grasped it in his hands and delivered it to her once more, his palm open. In the dream, they locked eyes and understood each other without words.

She awoke, sweating, her heart thundering with the rush of his presence.

He was never far away from her.

The arch of her ceiling was lit with thick buttery rays when someone knocked on her door. Ariadne finally startled from the dream's veil and slipped out of bed, grabbing a shawl, and draping it around her shoulders as she crossed her chamber. Before she granted him proper access, Advisor Cadmun entered with lengthy strides, his robes writhing like attacking serpents.

He bowed his head, and the sun glinted on his golden armbands. He wore many of those. Ariadne glared at him.

"Excuse you."

He ignored her protest. "Princess, the king and queen request you to join them." His focus remained on the floor, his dark curls shielding his expression from view.

She guessed that *messenger boy* was not his aspiration when he became the Advisor to the Palace of Knossos. Her interactions with Cadmun were rare, but she recognized his immense intelligence and ambition. Even now, bowed before her, she sensed how he itched for more.

She gestured idly. "Tell my parents I shall be with them soon."

He nodded and moved to depart.

"Wait," Ariadne said, something dragged her attention to a fine point.

Cadmun turned and briefly met her gaze. "Yes, princess?"

"Are the next sacrifices on their way?"

"No, princess. A person of particular importance arrives tomorrow. That is the primary topic their majesties would like to discuss with you."

She frowned. "Why would they discuss such details with me?"

He bowed deeper and said, "It is not my place to say."

Ariadne entertained the impulse to shake him upright and demand further explanation. Instead, she let him leave.

The invitation was unexpected. The king and queen had never before found a reason to ask for her counsel.

This must be something else.

As she peered into her mirror, Ariadne quickly assembled the visage of a princess. She braided her hair with swift movements, settled a small crown into place, and donned an emerald necklace. Two swipes of rouge on each cheek completed the facade.

"A princess must present herself impeccably," Ariadne recalled the queen once saying. Queen Aika intended the sentiment as a vital piece of wisdom, from royal mother to royal daughter. But Ariadne received the statement as a forecast of a gloomy future, one she was doomed to inhabit.

She slipped into a fresh gown and matching shoes, and laced the twine up her calves. Arranging her bodice, she straightened the wispy pale fabric and tugged the golden belt tight. With a brief scowl, Ariadne walked from her room into the bright hallway.

Through the half-circle windows, the placid sea sparkled as if trying to draw her focus. She did not look.

Ariadne's prison had no towering barricades or darkened edges. Ravenous crests lined the island, foamed and ephemeral and salty. She couldn't dwell on the ocean and what it represented without feeling unmoored.

Her soft shoes moved noiselessly on the polished marble, her pace quick and buoyant. Wind jostled the bright green vines adorning the archways. If the wind came from the east, she could hear the city's clamor and bustle, but mostly, the palace rested well above the clamor of others. Displaced, removed, all by design.

Passing the guards outside the throne room, she paused. King Minos could always sense her unease, using her emotions as weakness. He showed no cracks for her to leverage, no weakness of which she could take advantage. The queen always held something back, shielding her thoughts behind a mask. Ariadne had more success in maneuvering her, but only just.

The guards opened the doors at her nod, and she entered, lifting her chin.

"Mother, Father. I am here per your summons." She swallowed the bile rising in her throat.

"Thank you, Ariadne. I hope you slept well," Queen Aika said.

King Minos clasped his long pale fingers in his lap. "We have an important matter to share with you." He refused to refer to her by name.

Ariadne pulled her concentration from Queen Aika and onto her father. His white hair had thinned, and lines crowded his features. The man had no shred of fatherly kindness or wisdom in him. Ariadne had learned early not to expect such things.

"I see."

Ariadne allowed her attention to sweep the room. Advisor Cadmun hovered to the queen's right, hands folded in front of him, face guarded. She enjoyed being able to see his attractive features fully.

Of course, no matter how attractive he was, she would never pursue Cadmun. A man who chose servitude, even if it brought him closer to power, was contemptible.

"King Aegeus has sent a message that his son, Prince Theseus, shall arrive in Knossos tomorrow." The king stared at her, his exterior unreadable. Ariadne kept her expression placid, despite her mounting distress.

"Ariadne," Queen Aika said.

It was hard to miss the pinch of irritation Minos gave his wife at the interruption, but Aika ignored him out of habit more than obliviousness.

"Prince Theseus has volunteered to venture into the Labyrinth. He does it in your honor and plans to dispatch the beast for your hand." Aika spoke slowly, enunciating the words in her usual grandiose manner. Ariadne theorized this was a deliberate demonstration of her position that simultaneously disregarded the value of other's time. It was a subtle weapon the queen wielded. Too subtle, in Ariadne's estimation.

The king resumed his explanation.

"I have agreed to these terms with King Aegeus. Prince Theseus will enter the maze, kill the beast, and then return to his home with you as his wife."

Ariadne's mind stalled, like simple gears caught against their own jagged edges. Searing, molten rage quickly replaced this sensation. *No! How dare he make such plans for me?*

Drawing on her years of practice, she overcame the various twitches of rage running through her limbs, and repeated a routine internal refrain. *I command myself and direct my own way.*

"Yes, Father. I shall be pleased to meet Prince Theseus, and to see the beast's severed head on a platter the following day."

The throne room stilled.

"That is not the way a princess speaks," Queen Aika said, her warm complexion turning white.

Ariadne didn't fight the mad urge that seized her. "Would it be suitable for a prince?"

She dared to look at her father, who frowned, and refused to reply. She noted how Cadmun's eyes bore into her, searching.

Let them know I am no shrinking damsel. I too dream of victory and bloodshed, but not in the manner they have described.

Ariadne relaxed her shoulders and slipped into the shape of a smile. "Please excuse my enthusiasm, Mother, Father. I feel such joy at this news. The Minotaur's death and a betrothal is more than I could have imagined."

"Good. I thought perhaps you would protest the decision," Minos said. "You have always been a… *spirited* girl."

Ariadne's hatred crystalized, sharp and reflective. She briefly considered running forward to scratch the sneer from his face.

She borrowed Aika's technique and replied slowly. The words mattered less than her overall deference.

"I believe it is time I grow up, Father."

Minos stroked his largest ring—a ruby that mimicked death in its vivid hue—apparently satisfied by her deference. Ariadne swallowed. Rarely did she have a sense of triumph when talking with the king.

It felt good. Addictive.

Ariadne itched to escape the throne room, but Queen Aika gestured, and she allowed herself to be ferried to a corner. There, they were out of earshot of Minos and Cadmun.

"My dear, Prince Theseus is a brave man, handsome, and kind. I think he will prove to be a fine husband for you." She glanced at the king and folded her hands. "You are lucky to have a match worthy of admiration. You will find it easier to love him, too."

"I'm not sure I have your level of optimism," she said. "It's still against my will—"

Aika cut Ariadne off, her mask revealing a hint of something pointed underneath. "Oh, will is something we best not mourn losing." She straightened. "We will greet Prince Theseus together and your future will begin."

Queen Aika leaned in, bringing her hands to cup Ariadne's face. Her cool, smooth skin offered a rare and pleasant sensation. Ariadne stood firm, unsure of what Aika would say next.

"My daughter. So beautiful, so strong. This will be a good match, for you and our kingdom, though I will miss you."

Ariadne searched the green swirl of Aika's irises. There was a foreign gleam, a mimicry of sincerity or even its genuine form. Ariadne took Aika's lead.

"Thank you, Mother. We will each find a place in this new life."

They embraced, and Ariadne affected a weepy, breathless tone, sensing that was expected. Queen Aika sniffed, her own performance more convincing than Ariadne cared to acknowledge.

Chapter 2

Once her bedroom door closed behind her, Ariadne kicked and sent her shoes flying in different directions. She unclasped her gown with fumbling fingers. It puddled around her ankles, a delicate clump she stepped out of to pace the chamber.

She clutched at her chest and fought to expand her lungs, helpless even in her own body. A clammy sensation traveled down her neck as her skin prickled hot and cold.

Teeth grinding, she leaned against the wall and sank into the dread, thick and encompassing, a nearly physical assault that expanded. Despite her planning, her ideas and preparations, the river of fate had abruptly swept her into its current, pulling the most important decisions far beyond her reach.

The Minotaur killed, and the daughter married off. What a perfect outcome for the king.

Death and betrothal. Perhaps there was a sick amusement her father enjoyed in the circumstances.

She grabbed a shiny embroidered pillow and threw it across her chambers. There was a dull smack when it hit the wall, which was neither satisfying nor sufficient. Ariadne snatched another pillow and buried her face into its silken belly. The fluff muffled her outburst enough, but failed to decrease her mounting fury. She settled on ripping the tassels off the edge.

"These men discuss my life without regard for my wants or desires, let alone needs," she said through clamped teeth. "They underestimate me and for that, I'll rain destruction on them all."

Ariadne unclasped her necklace, the stone's pressure suddenly digging into her skin, and rested it on the table with a cold *clink*. Her hair fell to her shoulders in honey-hued brown as she removed the various clips. Absently, she combed the strands, glancing at herself in the mirror. The small crown on her head gave her the appearance of a princess, not a queen. A puppet to be maneuvered across the kingdom's board.

She tracked her nose, chin, brow. She sensed she was beautiful, had heard gossip about the multitude of suitors inquiring about the prospect of marriage, but she never saw them. King Minos preferred to send them away of his own accord.

But this new union benefited her father and his position. That was the only reason he accepted the offer. Prince Theseus, famed for his fighting skill and victories, would kill the Minotaur when countless others hadn't dared. Minos must be sure of that to agree.

Ariadne slumped onto her bed and traced the ceiling's mosaics. Her lids were heavy, but sleep wouldn't come. The situation threatened defeat, forcing her into a corner, depriving her of the best defense.

She thought of the Minotaur, how he had made no outburst in a whole day.

I wonder if he's all right.

On the orange glow of her closed lids, she saw him walking beneath the sun, planning his escape. Perhaps he merely needed help.

As I do.

The roles of princess and daughter sagged at her ankles like iron casts, promising obliteration. In response, she kicked and thrashed behind her closed door. Her parents could never witness her futile protests, nor could the servants. A princess must present a certain refinement in order to be accepted, but even these components of her appearance became a tool of her capture.

I am owned, decorative. I somehow must pretend to be grateful.

Ariadne sat upright, her jaw aching and temples throbbing. This was enough. The time had come.

She sat on her windowsill and plotted.

***

"King Minos beckons you, princess. Prince Theseus has arrived."

Ariadne didn't turn, from where she perched on the marble windowsill. From here, she could observe most of the Labyrinth. In a strange way, it soothed her to peer over the circuitous lines lurching back and forth, the angles and lines compacted tightly together. She traced the avenues like she had once tracked insect patterns chewed into leaves.

"Please tell my father I won't be long," Ariadne told her servant.

Terril bowed and left.

Rising to stand, Ariadne envisioned the Minotaur, an ongoing exercise that recently had shifted. No one living had seen him, she'd been told. As a child, she imagined him appearing large and friendly, similar to a dog she observed around the palace. Now, he looked different in her mind. He was colossal, fierce, and muscular. His expressions were haunted, and his eyes ravenous pits. The stories described his fangs, hooves, and horns, though how would anyone know? Hyperbole and fantastical additions. But Ariadne enjoyed these details and constructed her own. These were weapons she hoped to use.

The prospect offered a strangely flickering hope, an ember dimmed by soot but still glowing.

Ariadne rubbed her face and checked her reflection. The previous night was long and sleepless. She grimaced at the wan tint of her complexion and dabbed on a dusting of improved color.

I must make sure I am presentable. It would be such a shame to disappoint King Minos, especially on the cusp of leaving his house.

Several minutes later, Ariadne traversed the palace halls. She tapped her thigh to the rhythm of her steps, focusing on the rustle of exhale through her nostrils, the tickle of inhale on her lips. The high domes of the halls allowed planes of morning light to stream in, warming the smooth tiles under her feet. She fiddled with the intricate hem of her moss green dress. The splendor was a lie she would presently unveil.

Servants made themselves scarce, scurrying to their hidden rooms, expected to be invisible. They were the connective tissue that allowed this whole charade to run smoothly. To see them ruined the appearance, or so her mother had implied. Minos and Aika had shown Ariadne that to them, servants were barely people, with no importance or stature. They were there to support the king and queen, ornaments without autonomy.

All too soon, Ariadne arrived at the throne room, going rigid in front of the doors.

"Wait," she said to the guards.

They obeyed, and the doors remained shut, giving her a few more precious seconds.

In her pause, she considered the Minotaur in the maze once more, how his roars seemed to be made of grief, so pungent and visceral it rent the air. Someday she would permit herself to match the sound in savagery and duration. Her rage would converge with his, and he wouldn't be alone anymore.

We will transform his life of cruelty into that which truly terrifies.

Ariadne dropped her hand, and the doors swung open. She drifted, propelled by the unknowns of the past and the possibilities of the future. Her hands relaxed with effort, each step a deliberate decision.

She stood before King Minos and Queen Aika, awaiting their explanation, but it was someone else's voice that rang out.

"Princess Ariadne, it is an honor to meet you." A man materialized, dark boots clacking until he halted before her. He bent sharply, adjusting his sword so it didn't catch on the floor, and bowed.

Ariadne's gaze had been fixed on King Minos, thus failing to notice the newcomer when entering the room. She turned, recapturing her composure, and surveyed Prince Theseus. He dressed richly, his uniform suited for a royal and a soldier. Dark blue embroidery decorated his sleeves and collar, reminiscent of encroaching nighttime. He was pleasantly tall, features symmetrical and pronounced.

Prince Theseus straightened and met Ariadne's gaze. He was indeed handsome. Sun-painted skin and lightened hair told her he had spent most of his short years at sea.

She opened her mouth, but her mother spoke first. Ariadne guessed Queen Aika had misread her rigidity for social uncertainty. She forced her muscles to release their tension.

"Princess Ariadne, this is Prince Theseus, your champion and betrothed, should the gods deem him worthy of the task."

Ariadne swallowed and tilted forward in a bow of her own. "I am most glad to welcome you to Knossos, Prince Theseus. I am confident in your ability to rid our city of the Minotaur, and I will happily celebrate this success as your betrothed." Feeling the full weight of his focus, Ariadne allowed her expression to soften, which conjured a glint in his eyes in response.

He seemed naïve, overly sincere. *It will be simple to outwit him.*

"Thank you, Princess Ariadne," he said in a deep voice.

"This is a grand day indeed," King Minos said, standing and clapping his hands. "Prince Theseus, your courage and honor precede you. The Minotaur will be most affronted to encounter Prince Theseus instead of the expected group of sacrifices." He laughed. It was such a bleak sound; Ariadne shuddered.

Theseus appeared gratified as he turned to Minos. "You are generous with your words. I have trained for many years and know the stories. I will slay the beast without delay, King Minos."

"Of that I have no doubt. Tomorrow, we celebrate your imminent success with a grand feast." Minos regarded Theseus in a way that confounded Ariadne.

How quickly he seems to adore this Prince. Perhaps he sees the kind of son he's coveted.

Ariadne, dismissing the sickening knot forming in her body, stepped closer.

"Prince Theseus, we acknowledge and appreciate your bravery." Her stomach dropped, but she pushed onward. She looked at her father, keeping her body straight, and said, "If I may make a humble request?"

Minos raised his eyebrows and waited, signaling an accommodating mood. She steadied herself and rallied her confidence.

"I ask that Prince Theseus wait to enter the maze. For years, I have analyzed the Labyrinth from my balcony. I have an idea for how Prince Theseus may make his escape." Her fingers wrapped tightly around each other, bloodless from the force.

Theseus tilted his head at Minos, whose brow furrowed. Aika caught Ariadne's and gave a discrete bob of the head.

"Prince Theseus, what say you to her suggestion?" King Minos asked.

"King Minos, exiting the structure has always posed a larger challenge than dispatching the creature," Theseus said. "I would greatly appreciate any ideas Princess Ariadne can offer."

Everyone looked at her, and for the first time, she glanced at Cadmun. His eyes caught the light peculiarly. By the curve of his brows, she couldn't shake the feeling that he realized she was up to something. She tore her gaze from his and settled on Minos.

"If Prince Theseus approves, I see no reason to deny you. We shall reconvene after the feast and discuss further."

Queen Aika nodded. "Wonderful. Indeed, we have much to discuss."

"I am looking forward to the opportunity," Ariadne said. "If you will excuse me, I need to rest. Prince Theseus, welcome to Knossos."

He smiled. "Thank you, princess."

As she backed away from the throne, King Minos rose and approached Theseus. She could only guess what compliments Minos would give Theseus. Knowing herself to be already forgotten, she nevertheless bowed at the door, and bared her teeth once the doors shut.

Chapter 3

She had last left the palace unaccompanied six years prior.

It was a task for a son, she'd reasoned, hunting for food and glory. Ariadne had aimed to go out and catch dinner, to demonstrate her bravery. Of course, guards would always accompany a prince; she had gone alone and at night. Despite her demonstrated success in hunting, her parents were anything but delighted.

King Minos had punished her for a full week, imprisoning her in her bedroom and providing a single daily meal.

Queen Aika had visited her only once during this confinement, offering a brief consolation chased by a reprimand, more stern than Ariadne had ever witnessed from her.

"You are a princess, Ariadne, and you must act as one and use the tools at your disposal. Our tools are often invisible, yes, but they are vital for your survival, to achieve what you so desire. You mustn't try to be a prince to garner your father's respect. You know this will drive him further away, and myself. Is that what you want? To be without anyone in this life?"

Ariadne had found herself unable to respond.

The queen had not known love, at least not in her marriage, Ariadne guessed. And Ariadne renounced any claim to such a childish desire for herself.

She hovered by her door now, and suppressing the usual mass of distress caused by her mother's claim. Already, Ariadne lived in solitude within the palace walls, as the Minotaur did within his own.

She waited until after midnight, holding herself and waiting for the stars to shake the sky in their vastness. Finally setting out, she crept through the hallways in the delicate leather slippers that protected her feet from thorns and also eliminated any sound. Her breath became shallow, like a hand barely skimming a pond to avoid an outpouring of ripples.

This was a risk, she knew, but she had to meet the Minotaur to set each cog turning. There would be no more waiting.

A shadow stumbled down a different street nearby, someone drunk or lost. Ariadne brought her hood down on either side of her face and changed course to avoid them, taking a slightly longer route.

The city clustered across a low hill. The farther one traveled down the hill, the poorer the area became. Here, roofs gleamed dully in the moonlight, patched with various sections of rescued metal strips. Other debris cluttered the streets. It was irksome to see the needless squalor.

She had left her jewelry in her gilded box, but the gap under her collar bones prickled, as if she still wore her family's verdant emerald. If she sold it, the sum would cover several meals for many people.

Once, she had asked Queen Aika why the palace ignored their subjects' hunger. Aika had merely stiffened and looked to the horizon, her yellow tresses for once loose to brush her elbows. The absence of a reply dug a gaping pit into which Ariadne's mind fell. She had compassion in her heart, and a burning knowledge: if you provide everything subjects need, they will give you immeasurable loyalty.

If I am to take power, I shall offer them all reasons to remain loyal, and they will accept me without qualms.

Ariadne shook herself, passing what felt like countless houses and shops on her way to the Labyrinth. A sudden scattering sound made her dart behind a building, fearing a pursuer. Ariadne raised the edge of her hood and peered behind her but there was no sign of anyone following.

At last, her unease lessened, and she sprinted the remaining distance, her right hand holding the cloak at her throat. She came up short at the Labyrinth's edge, her heart thudding as she surveyed the blank impasse.

Moonlight pressed over the Labyrinth's surface, losing its beauty in the tiny crevices. There weren't any cracks or breaks in the exterior. The structure was a decade older than she was, but it defied age and degradation.

She tightened her hold on the cloak and readied herself to break the midnight quiet.

"Minotaur, I summon you," Ariadne said, and winced. Her voice rang frail and entitled. She hadn't practiced what to say. Her parents were seasoned orators and yet, when she most needed the gift of communication, language abandoned her.

She worked her mouth and tried again.

"Minotaur, I wish to talk with you." Pausing, she caught sight of a star arching downward, leaving a trail of bright, fleeting dust. It gave her a surge of confidence.

"I hope you can hear my voice wherever you are. Once, you heard me when I screamed, when I was desperate for anyone. It was you who came, though your identity was a mystery. This was some time ago." She guessed there was no purpose in describing exactly how long, if his days swelled together into a single intolerable mass. Or the opposite was true, and he marked each cycle of sun to moon with a claw mark on an otherwise empty wall.

Her feet shifted.

"You saved me from someone who wanted to hurt me. I shared my gratitude then, but it wasn't enough."

The ensuing hush wavered and grew, until it dwarfed her. She pressed nails to her palms, a sharp reminder of her aim.

Free the Minotaur. Free myself. And we will make our captors pay.

"I understand if you do not remember," she said. "Perhaps you can't hear me. But I will free you. This I promise. You won't be trapped for much longer."

Ariadne's blood seemed to halt in her veins when she heard a dense scratching. The presence heaved and shifted, like a great body rising from the earth. She leaned her forehead on the wall, listening harder.

A hoarse tone severed the stillness. "Go away."

She stepped backward, her newfound optimism withering. Then her anger flared.

"I am the Princess of Knossos. What did you say to me, Minotaur?"

He uttered a low growl. "Leave me. I am a monster and monsters don't save people."

The phrases tripped out of him, as if dragged, pummeled by his vocal cords.

Her offense dissipated, replaced by desperation.

"Please, even if you don't remember, I know the truth."

He made a noise more pained than amused. "Whoever you are, princess or not, you are wrong."

Shame took root and spiraled upward, sending tendrils along her limbs.

"Go."

By now, he seemed impossibly close, the vibrations reaching through the wall.

"No." She stomped her foot. "No, I have planned this. Together, we are going to change everything—"

"There is no together." His rasp punctured the air. "There is nothing here for you to save, princess. Don't come back."

Something rushed over her, akin to scalding water or frigid wind.

She couldn't put her feelings into words, much less sculpt a coherent response.

The pale white barrier stood between them.

She whirled on her heel and ran, the heavens a blurring disarray of light and motion in her haste.

**

Ariadne didn't sleep that night, nor did she eat the next day.

Doubt crept forth, stealthy and thick, until she could think of nothing else.

He won't help and he doesn't remember. I have failed.

Terril called from outside her bedroom door. "Princess Ariadne. If you'll allow it, I can assist you in preparing for tonight's feast."

This was Terril's third attempt to enter. Ariadne didn't want to see her parents, nor her servant, but time was short.

Everything must appear absolutely normal. I can't give anyone reason to question me.

She remained on the windowsill, eyes scouring the Labyrinth for signs of the Minotaur.

He had refused her offer, had denied ever saving her. *Perhaps I fabricated the memory that the Minotaur had called out.*

Memory was fickle and required exercising. She folded her recollection of that night, searching for the edges. The details formed, familiar and solid, yet she could no longer be sure. She had either convinced herself the roar belonged to the Minotaur or she had misunderstood his character.

She despised both prospects.

"Princess, are you awake?"

Ariadne released a sharp splintering breath. "Yes, Terril, I am awake. You may come in."

The door crept open and Terril entered, bowing. Ariadne looked out the window, massaging her tired eyes.

"I'm sorry for snapping and for refusing to let you in. You were just trying to assist me," Ariadne said.

"There is no need to apologize, princess. I am eager to be of service."

Ariadne bit her inner cheek. *No, you're not. Who would be pleased to help a girl throwing a tantrum?*

Whatever the gloom of her current mood, Terril didn't deserve such treatment. Ariadne walked to her chair and sat. Her form felt too heavy to match the ethereal beauty of the dress Queen Aika had given her for Theseus's celebration. She glanced over at the bed where the gown was draped, a frozen waterfall touching the floor. Terril rushed to pick up the length of silver fabric and smoothed the bottom over her arm.

Ariadne imagined whoever had crafted the dress couldn't rest until completing the task. Her own ruminations had made sleep impossible as she fevered over her plan, measuring other ideas. But she found no suitable alternatives, no options with sufficient benefits.

The Minotaur had rejected her offer, but she would make him see reason.

Terril coaxed Ariadne out of her daytime clothes—a loose dark shift suitable for lounging privately—and into the gown. The sleeves were open from the shoulders to her wrists. She watched as Terril scooped her hair into a braid, pinning it atop her head with pearls. Once subtle dabs of color adorned her face, Ariadne stood and felt the skirt dance along her legs.

"This is far too extravagant," Ariadne said.

"This is an important gathering, princess. Prince Theseus will soon be your husband, should the gods favor him."

Ariadne swirled her tongue in her mouth, the statement souring.

"Are you ready, princess?" Terril held a pair of deep blue shoes for her.

Ariadne smoothed the bodice and said, "Yes, I suppose I have to be." She slipped into her shoes and thanked Terril.

Her costume fully in place, she walked to the large hall where royal festivities were held. Bright lanterns lit the way and guards paced along the route. Her limbs trembled from lack of food. Another mistake.

I will require all my wits to navigate what comes next.

Guards observed her approach and ushered her into the hall. A dozen guests crowded the space, more than Ariadne expected. Her expression fell for a moment before she raised her exterior defense once more. Queen Aika appeared beside her, holding a glass of dark red liquid.

"Would you like some wine, dear?"

"No, thank you."

Aika sipped leisurely. "I cannot speak highly enough of Prince Theseus. He may not be the cleverest of men, but that is a benefit for you."

She spoke casually, as if imparting wisdom for how to host a large gathering of subjects.

"You mean it will be simple to manipulate him?"

"Indeed, daughter, and soon, you'll understand how beneficial that is." Aika's lips lifted in a secretive smile. "This will be your chance to use your gifts. You will shine, win over the people, and influence his rule. I imagined I too would have the same opportunities as a young woman." The queen took a deeper drink.

Ariadne searched for Theseus amongst the crowd. Instead, she located King Minos, who noticed her and lifted his drink. Throat drying, she saw Theseus settle beside Minos and engage him in discussion.

At their distance, she couldn't decipher the exchange.

"Mother, you gave me what you could, of this I'm certain," Ariadne said. "You have endured life beside Father, his wrath and control, and I admire that."

Aika's gaze softened as she said, "Thank you, dear. I have given you what is available to me with the privileges of my station."

You should have done more.

Ariadne looked to the floor.

"I am expected to converse with the guests. But daughter, I believe you will find satisfaction with Prince Theseus. You have a whole new life ahead of you. I envy that." Aika gripped Ariadne's arm as she spoke, then dropped it, turning to another guest.

Their conversation reverberated, a hypnotic thrumming that surrounded Ariadne. The guests didn't speak to her, and she let her gaze grow unfocused. In the distance, a dull roar slipped from the Labyrinth like smoke.

Chapter 4

People stirred at the sound of the Minotaur, but promptly resumed their discussions. This incensed Ariadne. Everyone at the dinner enjoyed themselves, indulged in rich foods and wine, as he wandered helplessly, awaiting his next meal.

She regretted not accepting a glass of wine.

Theseus appeared beside her, his broad shoulders perched too high.

"Princess Ariadne, you are radiant."

She blinked into the present, refocusing on Theseus. "Thank you, Princes Theseus."

He offered a subtle smile, the deep colors of his uniform melding into a rich tapestry of yellows and reds. She tasked herself with remaining beside him, soaking in his natural glow as if practicing for a probable future, seeing how it would fit to call him husband.

But all she thought of was the Minotaur and his jarring claim; "I am a monster."

Silence unspooled.

"I am grateful for this festivity and for the confidence in my success," Theseus said, after a time.

He shifted his stance, peering at Ariadne. When he paused, she pivoted toward him, providing a show of intentional listening.

"It is my belief we will soon care deeply about one another, as my parents do." Theseus's cheeks reddened. "As they cherish each other and their people, so too shall I love you and ours. Together, ours will be a union of happiness."

Ariadne swallowed. "There is no together," the Minotaur had said.

When her mouth opened, no words formed. Her thoughts floundered at his earnestness, and the room shut her in, swooping too close. She fidgeted.

I would use you, manipulate you, and you wish for love?

He grasped her hand and brought it to his lips, depositing a feather-light pressure. The brown of his irises poured into her. She withdrew her hand, shaking, and gave him a bow.

"You flatter me, Prince Theseus. I share your desires."

A bell rang out, signaling dinner. Theseus smiled fully this time, the vibrance of his teeth rivaling the gleam of his sword.

He believes me.

Theseus withdrew her chair, waited for her to sit, and guided the chair into place. She settled into the seat, aware of his focus upon her, and manufactured an interest in the table's discussions.

Despite her state of hunger, she maintained a slow pace during dinner. She spooned lumps of pomegranate when no one watched and chewed furiously. Her bites exceeded what propriety granted. A myriad of aromas accompanied the dishes on display, drowning her.

Her plate overflowed with the roasted meats and chunks of vegetables in variations and courses. Conversation grew louder as the guests drank more wine. Dessert arrived, a citrusy cake adorned with sprigs of mint. Ariadne gave them all the expected charming young princess. The additional guests, whose import she once deduced but no longer cared about, carried on a merry rumble into the evening.

For Ariadne, the feast moved slowly enough to be excruciating. Ariadne feigned interest in the flow of conversation, channeling her frustration into eating. She reminded herself more than once how patient she had been all her seventeen years. Another hour was nothing.

When King Minos stood, everyone quieted. He raised his glass and toasted Prince Theseus, offering a grand speech. But Ariadne wasn't listening. She saw how Minos stared at Theseus, the unmistakable excitement in his eyes. Anger swept over her like an excess of alcohol.

Theseus is the son he's dreamed of. And now he has him, a suitable heir. How I yearn to disappoint him once more when I overthrow him.

Before midnight, the multitude of guests thanked their royal hosts, congratulated Theseus, and filed out of the hall. It was an overwhelming tumult of limbs, voices, and chairs scratching on the floor, until only Cadmun, Theseus, Minos, Aika, and Ariadne remained.

"Now, you must tell us this grand solution of yours," Queen Aika said, addressing her daughter.

The three men in the room shifted toward Ariadne in unison. She smoothed the wrinkles of her gown, hands running the length of her thighs, and straightened.

"I have discovered a way to escape the maze, which is rather plain. I suggest a red thread."

"Simple indeed."

Minos's voice echoed between the walls of the dining room. The reverberation made him sound more aloof than usual, but something in his tone eluded her.

Ariadne stilled her vibrating limbs, considering the unfolding exchange with profound tact. Questions rose in her mind, so loud she feared everyone at the table overheard them. *Will he see through me? Can he guess what thoughts form in the darkness I hide out of sight?*

As Minos looked at her, his brows arched. Ariadne fought the urge to glare back at him. It took all her years of training, but her face remained composed and her tone benign.

"Yes, Father. A large ball that Prince Theseus will drop during his course into the maze, thus allowing him to retread the same path out of the Labyrinth." Ariadne ached from her stiff posture but ignored the discomfort.

The queen stared. To Ariadne's wonder, she actually looked proud. Ariadne turned to Minos, who reigned from the top of their dining table. His expression was unreadable and strange, as if the skin around his nose and mouth were long unused, unsure how to function. She almost thought he was on verge of smiling, and her heart clenched at the absurdity.

On impulse, she looked to Cadmun, whose countenance yielded nothing. There was a shadow of his beard appearing, and his gaze darkened. Her arms prickled with unease.

Ariadne understood Theseus at first glance. He appeared confident, strong, and kind, if overly sheltered. His unique combination of self-assurance and innocence charmed her, in a way. She eyed him and noted the set of his jaw.

I almost feel compassion for the man, for his painfully youthful and hopeful nature. How wrong he is about how this world operates.

Theseus leaned across the table, catching her in the brightness of his eyes, his intrigue too sincere to be theatrical.

"That is a fantastic solution, princess."

This man is ready to confront the Minotaur. A pity he will be too late.

"It is a fine idea," Minos said.

She had just enough poise to not react to Minos's comment, though she was stunned by this assessment. He rarely gave compliments, saving them for when all the other options for manipulating and cajoling had been utterly exhausted.

All attention rested on her, making Ariadne trip over her breath. A clink drew her focus back to the queen, whose glass glinted above her head. If they spoke, she did not hear them. The king, Prince Theseus, and Cadmun saluted her and drank. She mimicked the gestures woodenly.

A mass of feelings struggled for dominance inside. She had impressed them, and with such a simple solution to a problem. Her insides heated as if she stood too close to the fire and was burned for her folly. Then she reconsidered. It wasn't uncomfortable to bask in their accolades; in truth, it was what she'd always wanted.

Heat infiltrated her face. That such a small, positive reaction elicited this level of emotional turmoil made her heavy with shame. *How horribly sentimental.* The king had aimed to eliminate that weakness, and she had learned much from him. Soon, he would know how far she had come.

Theseus gave his thanks to King Minos, sent his gratitude to the cook, and navigated around the table. He hovered near her, but she didn't look at him. She watched as Cadmun leaned closer to the king and whispered into Minos's ear, suspecting the advisor was already sharing his opinions about the evening's proceedings. This posed a potential threat to her plan. However, she would be gone before Cadmun's interference disrupted anything.

Theseus cleared his throat, drawing her attention.

Pathetic. There were more important concerns than saccharine gestures and intimacy.

Ariadne inclined her head at him, and he straightened but didn't release her hand.

"Good night, Prince Theseus," Aika said, her voice forceful. At once, Theseus blushed, apparently noting that he'd held onto Ariadne for too long.

"Your majesties." He bowed and departed.

Ariadne moved to follow him through the doors when Aika intercepted her.

"Ariadne are you all right? You spoke little during the meal." Aika's concern conjured a bewildering series of emotions, one's Ariadne preferred to ignore.

"I am well, Mother. I am rather tired from today and anxious about tomorrow." Ariadne forced a smile.

"Of course. Rest well, dear."

"Until tomorrow," King Minos said. He glanced up from his conversation with Cadmun.

"Until tomorrow, Father. Cadmun," she said.

"Princess," Cadmun said with mock seriousness.

A rippling disappointment took hold as the seconds slipped by.

There was no name for her reaction, except perhaps regret. But that was baffling. She had never cared for them, and yet, on the precipice of leaving them, the landscape of her mind upended.

She swallowed and left the hall, her shoes thumping a soft percussion. Since she was a child, she had worked to harden her heart, to cultivate the traits that King Minos favored. He had achieved everything she desired; power and command, both for himself and over the residents of Knossos. But to her aggravation, a deep part of her craved something else altogether, craved what she had so infrequently received.

Ariadne entered the hallway, inhabited only by ghostly patches of thick moonlight. She removed her shoes, stepping on the cool stones, and swung them by their laces.

"When it is ultimately in my grasp, I turn into a simpering fool, melting at kind words and touches." Her exhale mimicked a hiss. She pressed her lips into a tight line, her fingernails curling into her skin.

A barrage of self-recriminations infiltrated, accompanied by a choking pressure in her torso.

Suddenly, a rasping howl cut the quiet, and she stilled only briefly.

The Minotaur. He was her future. He was in that maze, waiting. *As I have been waiting.*

Ariadne entered her chamber, stomach filled with acid and muscles taut.

Under her bed sat what she needed, out of sight until the last moment. She had packed it during the previous night, when she couldn't sleep.

By the time she heard the creature's resounding wail again, she was ready. Her emotions had settled, stray thoughts collected and subdued. Without a backward glance, Ariadne left the palace and stepped into the shadows.

Chapter 5

At last, Knossos was asleep.

Ariadne observed the dim, hushed houses lining the street, each containing someone capable of disrupting or entirely derailing her plan. There was no room for mistakes.

She peeked left and right, the hood draped low over her forehead. A dazzle of stars made the sky seem bolted in place, shepherded by a waxing gibbous moon.

Her attire was quiet by necessity. She wore pants and a shirt from Terril under the heavy cloak, and stalked quietly to avoid alerting others to her presence. She blended into the shadows, unseen and nameless.

When Ariadne first requested an exchange, Terril rejected any payment for the items. But Ariadne insisted, partially to avoid Terril getting in trouble for losing a uniform and partially to secure Terril's secrecy on the matter.

She crept through the city, keeping her elbows bent and toes light on the ground. When a hair-raising, guttural sound eviscerated the night, she froze. She hadn't been this close to him in many years, and the sensation thrilled her. It reached her ears differently there than on the palace hill. The maze deadened his roar somewhat, but she still detected the familiar raw, tremulous quality. For once, she began to tremble.

This was yet another shock. It occurred to her how easy it had been to inflate her own resilience, to assume she wouldn't be susceptible to the fear he so easily conjured in everyone else.

Or it was because he told me not to return.

Ariadne swallowed her trepidation and continued. After a few more steps, a loud rustling caused her heartbeat to gallop. She spun and spotted the culprit, a little cat running across the street.

Though she had expected it, panic still turned her body cold when the cavernous opening to the Labyrinth emerged. The walls rose over sixteen feet high. They were smooth, reflective, and ghostly in the moonlight. No sign warned passerby about this entryway. Everyone knew why these walls existed and what lived inside.

There was a tree standing nearby, an aged but solid tamarisk, one of hundreds that dotted the streets of Knossos. Ariadne tied the end of her thread on the largest branch and tugged hard. The branch shook, but the knot held, and she tied it twice more.

She focused directly in front of her, placing a foot before the other, and taking deliberate breaths. The dirt barely showed her light footprints. One, two, three steps. She kept going until she reached ten. She didn't realize for several moments she now stood inside the maze.

She halted, foot raised, searching every which way. The walls were sinister in their blankness, a taunt or a promise of the madness to come. She felt their indifference, their impenetrable stasis. Biting her inner cheek, dread slithered up her back.

The Labyrinth may reach over me, pull me down, and never let me out.

Ariadne shook her head. *No, I won't let that happen.* She had prepared for this. She glared at the structure and stomped deeper into the gloom.

She clutched the large ball of yarn and tightened her grip, the fibers tickling her skin. Ariadne altered her hold, allowing the string to unwind easily, and picked up her pace.

Hours slipped by like the red thread itself as she wound through the corridors. Twice she heard him, once near enough for goosebumps to erupt on her skin, the second round in the distance. She gritted her teeth and kept walking.

She had studied the maze from her windowsill for years, but being within the confines was more challenging than she foresaw. Lacking her previous vantage point, she struggled to navigate the corridors, having to turn back many times to find a different route. The awareness made her scoff. It was challenging on purpose. The real problem was having no sense of the Minotaur's location, and even if she discerned where he was, he might never stop moving.

Another possibility occurred to her; to call for him.

It was risky. Upon hearing her, he might kill her before she realized he was there. But that could happen if she stayed quiet, too.

Ariadne wondered about his possibly heightened senses, like heightened vision suitable for the dark. Perhaps he perceived the very presence of humans by smell. Otherwise, it would be difficult to track his meals in the maze. But he hadn't discovered her yet. It became ever more apparent how mysterious this creature was and how perilous her endeavor.

A new rustling intruded on the night, urgent and pronounced.

Ariadne froze and listened to the shuffling and a quiet rumbling groan. It didn't sound beastly. Perhaps it was a lost animal. Many animals, both pet and stray, had gone missing in Knossos, and most were likely victims of the Labyrinth.

Ariadne crept past another corner and jerked backward. She slapped her hands to her mouth to stifle a gasp. The ball of dwindling thread fell and landed in a cloud of dust.

A large mound loomed before her. It turned over and writhed, then settled. She watched the outline of the shape grow and shrink, finally concluding that it was asleep.

Ariadne forgot to breathe until a sharpness cut through her chest. With an excess of restraint, she pulled small parcels of air into her deprived lungs and their ache eased.

The shadow shape huffed and changed positions, breaking the spell.

"Hello," she said, shaking more than predicted. She rolled her shoulders and straightened as Queen Aika had taught her.

Movement shook the mound.

"Get away from me!" he said.

Ariadne recoiled, swaying side to side. She had to make him understand.

"I have come to free you."

A protracted pause. A lifted limb. Two orbs glinted in her direction.

"Why would a sacrifice free me?"

To Ariadne's horror, he stood in a rush of darkness and fabric. He towered over her, blacking out the moon and stars. His horns were caliginous smears. There was a weight to this void and she worried she would spill into it for an eternity.

Ariadne rounded her left hand into a fist, adjusted her posture, and surveyed him.

He looked like a human wearing a bull's mask. She discerned the lines of his cheekbones, the jut of his nose under a layer of thick reddish-hued skin. This bull visage ended at his shoulders, which flared out into long, chiaroscuro arms and a broad chest. He wore a black cloak synched at the throat and a cloth draped at his hips. She wondered, inexplicably, if he was cold. Unintentionally, she glanced down at his legs and feet, all in human form.

Perspiration beaded on her forehead, her fingers twisting together.

Ariadne realized the hush had grown too much when his nostrils widened under her scrutiny, his expression severe.

She considered running. *No, I must talk to him. I haven't come this far to give up.*

She stared at the Minotaur again. By his puzzlement, she gleaned he

29

wasn't used to people keeping their ground in his presence. A change flickered in his features, and he exhaled.

"You are not a sacrifice." His voice rasped from lack of use. "You are *that girl*."

His intonation somehow lashed worse than her father's ever had.

"I am the Princess of Knossos," she said, ignoring the wrench in her heart. "I am here to help you depart this prison so that you may exact your revenge on those who have kept you captive."

He scowled. "I told you already…"

"I am here to lead you from the Labyrinth and give you the power and respect you deserve. I will unleash you from your cage and your life will begin anew."

The Minotaur stepped backward. "What makes you believe this is a cage?"

The query flustered her. She opened and closed her mouth, attempting a response.

"You are trapped in this Labyrinth as punishment for a crime someone else committed, born of a human and a bull, left to this isolation and suffering. We can correct this wrong."

He stared at her so hard she shuffled her feet. In a flash, she understood she might die. She lacked the king's and queen's persuasive abilities and now her failure was unavoidable.

She fixated on regulating her breathing rather than the potential of her imminent and gruesome death.

"Born of a…?" The Minotaur broke off.

Of course, he's curious. I can use that to garner his loyalty. Or he would find the bribe of learning his own history a fine motivation to leave.

Recalling his claim of being a monster, she flushed.

Silence gestated while the Minotaur's eyes darted between hers. Whatever he was thinking, his thoughts seemed to change course as the seconds elapsed. He prepared to speak, and he didn't waver.

"You think living here for years, with nothing to do but wander, I never located the exit? That, at every corner, I don't know where it is? I remain here by choice, princess. This is where I belong."

Ariadne's jaw slackened, too overwhelmed by his words to reply. *But who would choose to stay?*

His features morphed, shifted, and she glimpsed who he was underneath. His eyes flashed, his prominent nose flared, and he appeared far younger than she would have guessed.

Her heartbeat tripped, as if needing to catch up after a prolonged pause. She steadied herself on the closest wall and considered what this meant. The Minotaur gave her an impatient, dismissive look and stalked down a corridor.

Several stagnant moments passed before his absence threw her from this stupor. She leapt after him, following the echoing *slap-slap-slap* of his bare feet on the ground.

"Wait! Minotaur!" Ariadne sprinted and reached him around the next corner. "You had the ability to leave all these years?" Confounded, she watched his torso rise and fall in a transfixing rhythm.

"I bring nothing but fear to the world. Can you imagine only experiencing the barbs of hatred?" He glowered, though she suspected his wrath wasn't directed at her.

Ariadne closed the gap to return the stare. He startled at the elective proximity.

"You are the most powerful creature in this land. You could bring King Minos to his knees, take the crown for yourself, force everyone to bow before you and refuse confinement. You could be free of this horror!" She had to crane her neck to counter his glare.

A curl swept onto his forehead as he peered down at her. She stared and another layer withdrew, like an apple from its peel. He leaned closer, hovering within inches.

He was within reach, and she almost extended an arm to touch him. Then he spoke.

"Power is not freedom." His tone was rough, as if he was trying to etch his meaning into her very being. He paused there, lingering to study her face, gauge her reaction.

Ariadne held firm, defensiveness overtaking her astonishment. With a swallow, she found her throat was too dry. She couldn't comprehend how he could be so wrong. She flattened her lips, and he severed their stand-off, snapping the tense woven string between them.

Without thinking, she grasped his forearm and the muscles underneath. The Minotaur flinched, regarding her with apparent suspicion. But instead of shaking her off, he went limp.

Ariadne burned with the dangerous act, encouraged by his supplication.

She loosened her grip, noting how his form responded. He curved inward, diminishing the gap further. She heard her blood thrash inside her ears.

Stop it. Whatever these feelings are, they are preposterous.

His attention burned, a fever that scorched.

"Power is the only thing that matters in this world," she said. "That is the way to control your own life, dictate your own future as you should. All those who have made you suffer..." She gulped, willing him to believe. "They can suffer in return. Now is your chance."

His upper lip curled, and he slipped out of her grasp.

"To you, I am only a monster."

Ariadne almost sighed.

"I think you are a king. You are worthy of more than you can imagine. I can help you achieve it."

He snorted. "No. You want to use me. Unleash the monster and reap what's left after the violence."

She paused, fascinated by his astute claim.

"Together," she said after a beat, "we can disassemble all of Crete and rebuild it to our liking. The gods will interfere, but we can fight them. Don't you see? We will strike down anyone who stands in our way."

Images flashed in her mind, of Minos falling, of expanding Knossos, of rejecting the gods. But the sight of him eroded everything else. He emanated a shade of sadness that pummeled her.

"I have lived my whole life in this place. Yet it is you I feel sorry for, princess."

He departed without another word, leaving her in a harsh and sullen silence.

Chapter 6

"What a waste of time."

Her nostrils flared as she stalked the corridors. "Another task I meet with failure." Each step conjured dust, a feeble protest from the ground.

I was a fool to let him in. I was weak.

The edges of Ariadne's eyes stung, moisture melting the white walls as she stomped the path. Her steps were loud and unsteady, but she had no energy to care. It was unlikely anyone outside discerned her presence, and if they did, they would never suspect the princess walked the Labyrinth's avenues.

Worse, however, was the secret part of her hoping the Minotaur would pursue.

What an absurd desire, an ignorant wish. I am as silly as ever, thinking he was my friend.

Her fingernails dug into the soft palms of her hands. She failed to stem the flowing disappointment, fresh as a cut. It originated somewhere deep and had nowhere to go, and she ached from the prolonged sting.

She gathered all the spite she had collected during her life, willing it to fuel her onward in overthrowing King Minos. But the raging mass flickered, changed, replaced by the Minotaur's warmth under her hand, the flare of his veins as he tensed. He held a bewildering contradiction of terror and terrorized. Someone whose exterior opposed their interiority, the monster versus the lonely boy.

Her cheeks heated. *I wonder about that boy, who he might have been, if it was he who saved me. I wonder if he's still in there.*

She stopped and glanced at herself. The cloak hung loose, her trousers sullied. Her attire was unusual, but that wasn't what winded her.

She felt a splinter of curiosity and care for him, beyond the useful. Her breath clattered in her lungs.

Father was right. I'm just a sentimental girl.

In a haze of anger, she had abandoned the much-dwindled ball of thread where it fell near the Minotaur. She tracked the line, grateful that following the blood-tinged chord posed no challenge. She rewound through the maze, weary and shattered.

I can urge Cadmun to help me overthrow King Minos. The notion was vaguely intriguing. It might have already occurred to him an opportunity to take control via the princess herself. She guessed he wouldn't require much convincing and she could think of worse husbands. She envisioned him, considered the almost viable alternative to the failed Minotaur plan. But she would have to share the throne, submit to equal rulership. She was not so desperate yet.

Theseus, then. He kills the Minotaur. I go back to his kingdom. Kill him one day and seize the throne. But Minos escapes unscathed. Her pace slowed, bloodlust diminishing.

She swiped at her brow, teeth gnashing against the tears. She refused to acknowledge them, refusing to nurse the wound the Minotaur had caused.

Instead, she wanted to hurt him in return.

I'll tell him of his origins, how his mother suffered. If he has any emotion in him, that will inflict sufficient pain.

She halted, dragging a hand across the wall.

Her voice sprang forth, frail in the quiet. "How like my father, I sound; cruel and selfish."

Ariadne clung to her cloak, succumbing to a wave of tears that rose, crested, overwhelmed. She invited them into consciousness, tasted their salt, and let them streak her face.

I cried that night until his voice broke forth.

Her thoughts returned to her previous plan after several more turns and an echoing call from the Minotaur. The timbre was concave and cold. It resonated in her bones and worsened the ache.

I should try again. I cannot leave him here, entirely alone.

There was something amorphous brewing that would only spark further confusion if she addressed it. Ariadne trembled from the Minotaur's words, a murmuring backdrop that pursued her. She feared that stopping for long enough would allow the legitimacy of his perspective to warp whatever resolve she still clung to.

"Power is not freedom."

With a gasp, she came to a halt and tried to calm the thunder of her heart. The rhythm made her grimace, like vicious waves upon rocks during a storm. Several attempts at deep breaths only left her dizzy. Thoughts clashed, demanding more focus than she could extend. Ariadne doubled over, clammy hands pressed against her temples to find a sense of order, of understanding.

In her crumpled heap, a single nauseating terror formed, sharp and inescapable.

What if what he says is true? I've seen what the king has achieved. His goal has always been to claim power. It's all that matters. Her eyes widened, a sob threatening to escape from a shadowed place within. In response, she shut them tight and ground her teeth.

If the Minotaur was correct—if destroying the king and defying the gods didn't satisfy her—she would have nothing else.

Ariadne envisioned him, resigned to his fate, crushed by loneliness. There was nothing in that life beyond suffering. And no one deserves to suffer without end.

Within her, a buried truth shifted, from diaphanous to solid, from distant to immediate.

A hint of pastel colors in the east caught her attention. Time was slipping away as the sky inexorably rotated. The hours dwindled and with them, her only chance.

Her legs began running before she noticed. Her blurred vision made hurtling around corners difficult, but she didn't slow down.

I have to convince him, persuade him, if solely for his own good.

The stars glistened overhead, neutral and unconcerned, fading into the brightening sky as the sun coalesced along the hidden horizon. The telltale sounds of Knossos waking up crept over the Labyrinth walls.

She ran faster. Thirst rattled her, but she denied the base need. The most important thing was finding him. Rescuing him.

As someone rescued me once. Perhaps it wasn't the Minotaur who saved her, but that wouldn't stop her from helping him escape the Labyrinth.

She followed the red line around a bend, and slammed into a dense mass on the other side. The impact sent her sprawling, and a remote pain flourishing behind her forehead gave the impression of an abrupt fall.

Her vision filled with a half-man, half-bull crouching over her as she slipped into oblivion.

Chapter 7

Ariadne startled awake, prickling from nausea. Her body smarted in multiple areas, which all screamed for her attention. Her head throbbed viciously, and she was strangely heavy, arms draped on her stomach. A hip was jarred and sore. She shifted to relieve the pressure and shut her lids against the burn of bile.

She laid still, panting slowly, and waited for it to pass. She saw the Minotaur crouching close by, wearing another unreadable expression. She stiffened, then sat upright, feeling too vulnerable before him.

"Slowly," he said, arm shooting upward, and letting it fall at her stern expression.

"What happened?" She adjusted herself on the hard ground, and the exertion made her groan. He lurched forward at the sound, and Ariadne brushed off his gesture.

"You will answer my question at once."

He relented with a shrug. "You ran into me, bounced into the wall, and fell. You were unconscious for a few minutes." The line of his jaw pulsed as he studied her. "Why did you come back?"

Not ready to answer that question, she asked, "Why did you spare me?"

She searched his large and frenzied gaze, his eyebrows bunching.

"I have only killed a single person." He fidgeted as he inclined on the opposite wall.

"Then how have you stayed alive? Where are the sacrifices if you didn't kill them?"

The Minotaur look shrouded, as if he was attempting to appear emotionless. "Some killed themselves, some each other. Others died from thirst, starvation. I took that initial life, thinking it was the only path to survival. Everything after that... I simply encountered what remained."

Ariadne recoiled at his implication, and shook her head, desperate to fit the jagged and disparate pieces together. *He ate what he could without causing harm.* This claim opposed everything she had learned about the Minotaur. But when she studied him in the pastel shadows, she saw a raw, unfamiliar honesty.

She tracked the plains of his face, searching for comprehension. Already his human features overpowered that of the bull. And within their details, she observed the many wounds he endeavored to conceal, the mourning and regret.

Empathy. He has empathy.

He shot her furtive, fretful looks during her inspection.

Steadily, she unveiled him, as if removing layers of clothing. *He has chosen exile and suffering because he believes his existence warranted that. He has no intention of injuring anyone.*

"So you are not a killer?"

An aggressive flush reddened his cheeks. "No. Though I imagine no one would believe me."

"You should have told me before."

"What does it matter? Unless..." He stopped, countenance tightening.

She eased the weight off her hip, uncomfortable with his possible insight.

"You wanted me to hurt someone for you," he said, almost inaudible.

"Since you are not what the stories say you are," she said, trying to cover her guilt, "why do you stay here?"

He jumped to his feet. "Look at me!"

Ariadne reared back in surprise and once more collided with the Labyrinth wall. His posture of frustration immediately deflated and he slumped once more, his attention devoted to her alone.

"I am all right. Or will be eventually," she said, rubbing the rising bump on her head.

He nodded, but concerned wrinkles spiraled across his features, his unease compounding.

She absently rubbed circles on her arm and asked a question with the hope it might distract both of them.

"What is your name?"

"I do not have one."

"How can you not—" She broke off, reading his dejection. In response, her heart twinged, a most disconcerting new habit. Though she thrummed with pain due to her injuries, she moved to sit beside him, the Minotaur watching warily.

Ariadne settled on the ground, letting her knee rest a hand's breadth from his. "Is there a name I may call you?"

He squinted and looked down the corridor to the right. She didn't press. Some part of her knew he would answer when he was ready. Her patience was rewarded after several long moments.

He looked at the sky, mouth opening and closing for a time. "I... once heard a person outside, near the edge. The voice was high and—" A muscle jumped in his jaw. "—loving. It said 'Aster, dinnertime!'" His throat bobbed as he hazarded a glance in her direction.

"Aster is a good name."

If the light were more generous, she guessed she would see the full extent of his relief. But in the gauze of morning, she sensed how he relaxed. She followed, her shoulders loosening, easing closer.

"Is it childish to be this happy when shown kindness?" He glanced over, to witness her rejoinder, or perhaps to confirm that she hadn't vanished.

"This I can relate to. Before yesterday, King Minos never once complimented me," she said. "And I had never seen the queen so proud and it made me... happy, I suppose."

"And your name, princess?"

For once, the moniker didn't seem forced or belittling. "Ariadne." She grinned, as did he, revealing tentative dimples. The exchange shot tiny flares of excitement through her limbs. He appraised her, but when she did the same, he pivoted to pick at the dirt.

They sat in silence and reality congealed, becoming tangible, unavoidable.

The plan to overthrow King Minos lay fragmented at her feet, ruined. She mourned her failure. Her sustaining rage had cooled, replaced by shaky sadness. All such emotions she buried far below, as her training required.

Aster dragged a finger through the dust, making a line parallel to her leg.

"I can tell you your origins, if you would like," she said.

I will offer this freely, with no ulterior motive or demand.

He didn't move, didn't speak. But his eyes were round with a guarded anticipation. In his lap, his fingers were tangled and bloodless.

"It began with Poseidon, god of the sea," she said. "He sent a white bull to be sacrificed by the people of Crete. But, foolishly, the old king decided it should live. Poseidon was quite angered by this disobedience."

Aster took in each word with brows creased and lips parted.

"In his anger, he punished the King by making his wife fall in love with the creature. Upon their union, the queen became pregnant."

"And after that?"

"The wife gave birth but couldn't bear it, and took her own life. The king, weakened by the affair, was overthrown by my father, Minos. One of his earliest commands as the new king was to construct the Labyrinth. You grew rapidly. You appeared... already self-sufficient, so no one cared when Minos cast you inside its walls so soon. Of course, I doubt anyone would have conjured any further compassion for a baby."

There was no way to cushion the delivery, to avoid the brutality of his origins. He trembled, his features at war between grief and anger.

In observing his reactions, confusion struck her. Aster was, by every conceivable parameter, to be feared and avoided. A threat unleashed on Earth by the gods. But she placed a hand on his knee, compelled by something unidentifiable to offer comfort.

He blinked, focused on where she touched him.

"I, too, know my origins. My father, the king, wanted a son," she said. "I was born a disappointment, but still I tried to make him proud. None of my attempts were enough. My mother wishes for me to accept the meager tools at my disposal, to find satisfaction in this. She doesn't understand and she never will. I have long known they will never accept me as I am. Perhaps you would have preferred not knowing. I cannot say which is better; to learn the truth or to stay ignorant." She swallowed and tightened her grip on his knee. Under her pressure, his shaking gradually abated.

"I thank you, princess. I have longed for understanding." He craned skyward, exposing his neck. "Over the years, I constructed many stories. I came up with endless reasons and excuses to explain to myself." He gave her a sideways look. "Ariadne, I'm sorry you are... unwanted by your parents. That you must, somehow, be different. You are carrying your own disappointment. I see it."

She withdrew instinctively. Her role as princess required her to mask her feelings, to hide her truth out of sight. And yet he observed her, detected all that she secreted away.

"I do not desire to avenge any wrongdoing of my past," he said. "But the rejection you've experienced... That I wish I could change."

Aster rested his hand on hers and she let him.

It seems I was right; he is a friend.

Locking eyes, she believed he almost smiled, but the expression passed quickly.

"Thank you for returning, Ariadne. I am glad to see you again. But you must leave the Labyrinth." He straightened and offered his hand.

She accepted, her jaw slack from his discomfiting shift. The heat of his skin sent the sensation of tendrils shooting along her palms and up her forearm. She wondered how it would feel to cup his cheek. He released her, but she gripped him harder.

"Aster, I can't deny that I came here with the wrong assumptions about you. For that, I am deeply sorry. Now… Let me help you. Please leave with me and we will go anywhere. Imagine somewhere you'd feel safe. *Anywhere* and we'll make our way."

He stood absolutely still, limbs loose, eyelashes glistening. "Your whole life you have seen me as a monster in a cage. You do not know me." His voice rasped, like wind in brittle branches.

"That's not true! You have never experienced elation or contentment, and you deserve to. And, Aster, I want to help." She panted, spurred on by clarity. "I have only ever made decisions for myself, to reach my own objectives. But with you…" Her words caught.

He pitched his upper body down, searching her face as lines spread on his brow.

"It's wholly correct to consider you, to defend you," Ariadne said. "I cannot explain it, but I don't think I need to."

His expression of bewilderment almost made her laugh, but she stifled the impulse.

This is what we both want. He must understand that as I do.

Nascent rays of sun splayed across his dark hair. Ariadne brushed the series of tendrils from his forehead, gentle and tentative. He leaned into her touch.

She warmed, confident he would leave with her then. That she had convinced him, that they would go together.

"You are baffling and beautiful," he said.

The compliment was like the first gust of spring air after winter. A surge of chaotic glee followed, causing her to sway, and his arms encircled her.

"I will come with you," he said. "But we must move now. It could be too late. The prince will be coming."

She went rigid. "You heard of the prince and his mandate?"

"I overhear all kinds of things."

"He will not kill you."

A beat of silence, and he whispered, "And what if he should?"

Ariadne twined her fingers through his. "There is no should, Aster, for fate does not confine our choices. Come." She presented her hand, palm open. "I know the way."

Aster snorted. "And you claim I do not?" He allowed her to tug him along the red thread, leaving the bowels of the maze behind.

They didn't make it far before another call sliced the air.

Prince Theseus stood in their path. "Princess, move away from this dangerous beast. I come to kill the Minotaur."

Chapter 8

The ground seemed to drop away.

We have run out of time.

"Prince Theseus."

Dread eviscerated her recent joy. She stepped toward Theseus, conjuring every ounce of Queen Aika's conviction. "He is not what you think he is! I give you my word he is not dangerous."

Theseus frowned. "Of course he is, princess. I ask you, please, to depart the Labyrinth. I do not want you to be hurt." He closed the gap, sword outstretched. With each step, the blade reflected splinters of light peeking over the Labyrinth's walls.

Panicked, Ariadne grabbed hold of Aster, positioning herself between him and Theseus. Aster immediately gripped her, rearranging their positions so she was now behind him. Ariadne yelped, stumbled, and righted herself as Theseus halted. She craned around Aster's frame to address Theseus.

"I command you to stop this, Prince Theseus. Aster poses no threat to anyone, especially me."

"Aster?" He frowned, then rolled his shoulders, as if to dismiss his bewilderment. "Here in this horrible place, you cannot command me, princess. The king has tasked me with killing the Minotaur. This is his fate and my destiny."

Outrage and disgust churned her stomach. She wouldn't let Theseus's supposed destiny upturn her own. Not after all that had transpired.

Prince Theseus positioned himself for the attack.

Ariadne threw herself against Aster's arms, spitting rage.

"If you want to hurt him, you'll have to hurt me first!"

Aster shielded her, arms clenched, and eyes wide.

"You cannot kill him!" Her voice splintered. "He is not what we have always been told! He is kind—"

Aster interrupted her with a restrained, fluid push, casting her out of striking range, and Theseus seized the opportunity to dispatch a blow to Aster's head. Aster blocked with his arm, grunting at the impact, as blood splashed grotesquely onto the dirt. From her position, she watched each drop splatter on the dirt.

A brutal fear seized Ariadne. She stilled, unable to direct her limbs.

The time for profound action had arrived, and she was impotent.

I must act. I claim to want to help him. My chance is almost gone.

Under the sharpening sunshine, Aster grasped Theseus's wrist and overpowered him, forcing Theseus backward. Theseus regained his footing and shoved the blade deeper into Aster's arm. Staggering, Aster clutched the wound and gritted his teeth. Theseus pushed forward, undeterred by the damage or Ariadne's frantic protests.

"Theseus, I beg you, please don't do this. He is innocent!"

That disrupted Theseus's focus. He balked and glanced at Ariadne. Aster's chest heaved, but he remained motionless, ignoring the worsening blood loss.

"Innocent? How can you say that? Why are you defending this monster?"

"He is not a monster." She summoned all her remaining composure. "He only killed the first sacrifice. Please believe me. He is a good man."

Theseus stared at her with compassionate condescension, as if she was a child who lost her way. "You have gone mad."

Ariadne released a growl. The details of her physical wounds were long forgotten, but the effects continued. She separated Prince Theseus and Aster, woozy but determined.

Theseus studied her until his expression softened. "Soon, I'll bring you from here and all will be as it once was. Trust me, princess." He lifted a gentle hand to Ariadne's cheek, making her twitch out of his hold. "Whatever happened to you while lost in the maze, you will recover."

"No! You do not understand—"

"I have a duty to fulfill," Theseus said. "Even if that means I return without you as my bride."

At the statement, Aster turned to stare at her, and she floundered for a response. There in his dark eyes was a delicate thing in the process of shattering.

"Ariadne." The utterance made her heart falter. Aster pursed his lips. "Thank you for your optimism. But there was never any other future for me. Please leave. You mustn't witness what comes next."

She could barely discern his outline through her ferocious tears. They gathered on her lashes and spilled as she stood up, seconds suspended between the three of them. Taut to the point of snapping. Her heart squeezed like clay in a vise.

She curled her fists, turning to Aster. "I won't leave you," she said between breathless sobs. Beneath the fear and desperation, there was shame, horror, confusion. Thoughts whirl-pooled in her mind; *How did I become someone I cannot recognize during a single night? Someone who loves, who has hope?*

"You must."

"No," she said and moved in front of Aster.

Theseus startled. "Princess, the beast speaks the truth. You do not belong here." But he sounded less certain. He had witnessed Aster's refusal to defend himself, taking Theseus's blows without fighting back. He had seen Aster's insistence that Ariadne leave.

I can use that. She straightened, gathering the tattered strips of her royal training, and confronted him in an even tone.

"Prince Theseus, you are noble and compassionate. You believe in love and honor. Do you see how thoughtful this man is, how he means neither of us harm? He won't fight you because, after his years of profound misery, he thinks death is all he deserves." Ariadne wiped the last of her tears, and poured whatever she had left into the next words. "I came here to release him, to destroy everything I have ever known. Now, I want to join him in search of a better life. Do you not see the miracle of that? Is it not wondrous?"

Theseus lowered his sword. She pushed on.

"He was left here to suffer unimaginably and has no unnatural powers. He knows the way out and yet he stayed here. Theseus, I assure you, Aster has suffered enough. Do not add more because of a misplaced sense of honor and responsibility to a power-hungry king."

Theseus's eyes swung to Ariadne and then Aster. His conviction wavered. He might not grasp the complexity before him, but she sensed he wouldn't condemn a creature in his uncertainty.

"I cannot comprehend what has happened, nor do I think I wish to. But if what you say is true, perhaps killing him is neither necessary nor just." Theseus sheathed his sword.

Ariadne didn't dare breathe, not sure if she heard him right. Theseus scanned Aster, who was so still as to be carved from marble.

"Can you promise you won't harm anyone again?" Theseus asked. "That if I spare you and let you escape, you won't be a source of brutality?"

Aster swallowed. The morning light cast his face in half-glow, half-shadow. "I cannot assure you of what will come to pass. But I say honestly that I am dedicated to avoiding violence and death at my hands, and I commit myself to this for all of my remaining days."

The words were steely and resolute. She stepped closer, forgetting Theseus's presence. There was only Aster cast in the purple-orange-yellow sky.

In the ensuing stillness, Ariadne felt something stirring, expanding, rising. None of this was what she had expected but it was like returning home after thinking she had none.

We will be free after all.

Aster stooped to Ariadne, holding her in his auburn gaze. It was as if he observed her resentment, jealousy, greed, and ambition. He saw everything she was. And he smiled, wide and wild.

Suddenly, she remembered Theseus. She turned to him, observing his agitation. But he didn't raise his sword.

"I will let you go," Theseus said. "I can accept that King Minos summoned me here under false pretenses, that the Minotaur was a monster who needed to be slain. That is inaccurate, if I trust what is witness here, and it would bring dishonor to kill you, knowing this."

The air itself grew more lithe, or perhaps it was Ariadne. She leapt upward and Aster caught her, wearing a dazed grin. His arms went around her torso, pulling their bodies flush, and her feet dangled by his ankles. Laughter escaped her, buoyant and heady.

"Aster," Ariadne said against his neck. He squeezed her harder, fingers layering the bones of her ribcage. She burned at the touch and yearned for more.

Theseus cleared his throat, and Aster lowered Ariadne to standing. Pink swathed Aster's cheeks, mirroring the clouds. She pictured a similar shade dusting her own.

"You must run before I reconsider... And before all of Knossos awakens. It would be unfortunate if the princess was seen running away with the Minotaur." Though Ariadne guessed Theseus had good intentions, she dismissed his worry.

"I do not care who sees," she said. "I care only that no one hurts him."

Aster offered her an incredulous look, the expression both endearing and entertaining. She squared her shoulders at Theseus, feeling stronger.

"Thank you, Prince Theseus. You deserve to rule Knossos, not Minos. He will lose his power once everyone discovers the Minotaur has escaped and I encourage you to consider taking his place. You would rule with the same generosity and compassion you have shown us here today."

For a disconcerting moment, she almost felt Queen Aika's voice speaking through her, guiding the words out of her mouth to occupy the Labyrinth's pathways.

Theseus pressed a palm to his chest in acknowledgment. Then he said to Aster, "I suggest you wrap that." He bowed to Ariadne, and dashed away.

Ariadne watched him go, giving him a head start. Hurriedly, she tore the bottom strip off her cloak. "He's right. We should stop the bleeding."

Aster presented his forearm, the blood beginning to dry near his elbow and wrist. The gash itself seeped rather than gushed. She wrapped the wound and pulled the fabric tight, hearing the hiss slip past his lips, but he didn't flinch. Tying the two ends, she patted the wrap and met his gaze.

"Are you ready to depart the Labyrinth?"

He gaped at her for a moment, but gave a firm nod.

They ran as one, clasped hands swinging between them.

Chapter 9

Despite her lack of sleep, Ariadne seemed to fly as fast as Aries himself. Aster dashed ahead of her, slowing his pace, and glancing over his shoulder every few seconds to make sure she was with him.

If only I had greater legs, he wouldn't have to slow down. Still, his awareness of her and accommodation conjured a foreign joy. She raced on, allowing her excitement to pump energy into her tired, quaking muscles. The red thread guided them like a trail of dried blood out of the maze.

They heard the acoustics of Knossos, loud and routine. She couldn't guess how the villagers would react when they saw them. Aster eyed her, as if sensing her thoughts.

"Where will we go?" He didn't sound winded in the least.

Gasping for air, she said, "I presume you never learned how to swim?"

"I haven't had the pleasure."

"Then we must use a boat, cross the sea, and go somewhere no one will find us." Each word came out clipped. "We build a life far away."

They rounded another corner and came to an abrupt halt. The opening of the Labyrinth opened before them, revealing the houses beyond. Aster trembled, and he swung his hand to grasp hers.

"Are you all right?" She laid a palm on his chest. His eyes jumped between her and the exit.

"Yes, I cannot explain to the extent that I am. I never dreamed I would be so... all right." He blushed and let his head fall.

She lifted his chin, raising his gaze to hers. The facade of the bull had faded hours earlier. She saw only him, a man stretched between gods and mortals. And a brazen whim took root.

Ariadne lurched to her tiptoes. Aster swayed and steadied, clasping her elbows, and squeezed gently, a nod bringing him nearer. She kissed him and light blazed on her closed lids.

His lips responded slowly at first. But soon he touched the space between her shoulder blades, hands clutching tight, then lacing through her hair. His hands moved to press her into his torso and she surged higher still. His bracing was for both of their sakes, she guessed.

She pulled back, swaying in his grasp, as Aster broke into a wide smile. He released a small noise, which she concluded was a chuckle.

"We shall have more of that soon," Ariadne said in a wispy, unfamiliar tone. There was a flavor of command and desire in her words. He looked abashed but eager, a combination she identified intimately now.

Without further delay, she drew him into the world he was never supposed to inhabit.

They tore through the last of the gray corridors and into the streets beyond. A cacophony of yelps engulfed them, but they barreled through, undeterred. Crowds parted, bodies scrabbling to dodge the perceived peril. Shock and terror made most of them scurry into their homes.

"We go to the dock. The king prepared a ship to include in my dowry. I do not think he will miss it," Ariadne said.

Aster showed no signs of hearing her. He captured glimpses of the city he had listened to and never seen, observing all he could in haste. More people screamed, but none stood in their path. No residents were that brave, or that foolish.

They maintained their pace, though Ariadne would later question how they had managed it. She led them hastily, for daytime was upon them. Sweat prickled on her brow and she unbuttoned her cloak, letting it waft to the ground. She glimpsed a child with black hair scrambling after it, their mother shrieking.

Ariadne laughed. *I hope you find that cloak as useful as I have.*

The voices faded as they reached the outskirts of Knossos, and to her wonder, she rejoiced to witness the ocean. The tranquil waters beckoned, their hue serene. What she once thought was another layer to her confinement, she now realized would be the very function of their escape.

It took a quick glance to identify the correct ship. What it lacked in size, it more than made up for in regal design. The vessel had a tall mast, an intricately decorated prow, and snapping sails.

Unable to speak, Ariadne pointed at it. Aster nodded, then swept her up and carried her to the ship without faltering. She jolted with surprise and circled his neck with her arms.

Above them skipped a plethora of white clouds on a westward journey. Diaphanous water reflected a dazzle of minuscule points surrounding Crete. Trees shifted in the breeze, as restless as Ariadne herself.

This is the moment. This is everything I have been reaching for my whole life.

She peered at Aster, noting how his dark hair plastered to his skin from exertion. Yet his expression was open, reflecting the glinting water. He kept running but glanced at her, eyebrow raised.

"You're not accustomed to being seen," she said.

Aster's steps faltered, but he didn't drop her, and she knew he never would.

"I'm not used to any of this. But yes, a princess staring at me is by far the strangest occurrence."

She grinned, and he gradually joined her, his whole being bursting into happiness. A dimple appeared, tucked into his bronzed skin. She traced her lips there, and the indentation deepened.

Ariadne didn't notice they'd arrived at the dock until he moved to lower her. She considered protesting, but his form had stiffened. Frowning as he released her onto the waxed planks leading to the boat, she realized the mirth had drained from his body.

"Aster, what is the—"

He grunted and gestured toward the sea, fingers curling into fists. She whirled in the direction he indicated, and her heart stopped.

The boat wasn't empty. Someone was already on board.

***

"You have always managed to surprise me," King Minos said.

The dictate evident in his tone confirmed that this was not a compliment.

He halved the distance between them, his long, maroon-colored vest swinging around his black boots. "Few people have accomplished the feat once. This is the only realm where you seem to excel."

Ariadne ground her teeth. Behind Minos, Aika hovered, face pinched and ashen.

I've freed Aster. And myself. We're so close and yet my parents once more stand in my way.

Minos rubbed his largest ring. "Here you are, daughter, standing there with the beast that should be dead. I dislike being surprised. And as your primary habit, I find it aggravating."

Aster growled and placed himself between Ariadne and her parents.

"Now, now, look at this perplexing creature." Minos strode across the dock, Aika in his wake. "The Minotaur, who I have conquered, who Prince Theseus set out to kill, defiant in my presence."

"Minos," Aika said, her voice a sharp warning.

"He will not hurt me, wife. I am aware of his behaviors. He has never killed a sacrifice. Except for one, when he was young and hungry."

Aika gasped.

Ariadne shoved past Aster, glaring at her father. "You knew he didn't hurt anyone. That he was peaceful and still you wanted him dead—"

"He had served his purpose. My reign was secured and, perhaps, I tired of the Minotaur. Hadn't you noticed how quiet he has been of late? He was seemingly dying of his own accord."

Imagining Aster losing himself in the maze split her heart.

"I should have guessed," she said, cutting the distance to Minos. "The people wouldn't be afraid anymore and Theseus's success would mean you'd be rid of me and gain a son. The Minotaur was only a ploy to you, as he was to me before..." Her throat dried.

"Ah, so you are of my blood, after all. Let me guess," Minos said. "You planned to use him to overthrow me."

Ariadne worried the interior of her lip, her confidence curdling.

"A rather weak plan, but I applaud your ambition. Or your intended ambition. You plan to flee Crete now, is that correct? You have found love with this monster?"

"He's no monster!" Rage swirled in her mind as vertigo descended. "You're much more vile, abhorrent, and despicable than he could ever be."

Aika appeared, separating them. Her pale skin shone and lines of tension gathered from her frown. "Ariadne, you just met this creature and cannot trust him! It is not better to be with an evil you know than an evil that is unknown?"

Minos scowled at Aika, who merely straightened. She wouldn't shrink before him and she never had.

"It's better to leave evil behind," Ariadne said, taking Aster's hand.

"And you're wrong," Aster said. "She knows me."

"Absurd," Minos said.

"I didn't want her to. I told her to stay away, but she is stubborn." He looked at Ariadne, lips tugging upward on one side.

Minos scoffed. "On that, we can agree."

"I'm not finished," Aster said, muscles tensing.

King Minos withdrew a step.

"As a child, she ventured by the Labyrinth," Aster said. "I don't know why, but someone threatened her. She called, and I frightened them away. At that moment, she thanked me. Later, she visited again, promising to free me. She knew my deepest desire was to no longer feel alone. And she came back over and over."

Minos's upper lip curled, nostrils flaring. "You are as pathetic as she is."

"Your insults don't wound me anymore, father," Ariadne said.

Minos laughed, a sound akin to vitriol rather than amusement. "I shall summon Theseus. The piteous lad is likely lost in the Labyrinth. Perhaps he isn't as bright as I'd hoped. Nevertheless, he shall kill you in front of my subjects like the obedient boy he is—"

"King Minos, forgive me, but I will do no such thing," Theseus said, stepping onto the dock

The tendons in Minos's neck jumped. "You failed, prince. The Minotaur is here and claims your prize as his own."

"I didn't stop them, and I heard your words." Theseus raised his sword.

"That is hardly an achievement." Spittle flew as Minos spoke. "You have ears but no brain, it would seem."

Undaunted, Theseus said, "You are unworthy of your throne."

A streak of panic contorted Minos's mouth. He whirled toward the boat, yelling at the man on the prow. "Sailor, I direct you to take this ship away this instant!"

The sailor glanced at the king, his brows stitching. "Aye, King Minos." He released the sails, and the boat leapt away from them, the gap of water widening.

Ariadne's rush of glee at Theseus's courage crumpled. The boat pushed farther out of reach. Aster took her hand, his fingers twitching as if to say, *be ready.*

Aika walked to stand beside Theseus.

"He's right about you," she said to Minos. "They all are. I've accepted what I have, used the power I yield, and never confronted you. That changes now."

The boat was several yards from the dock now. Everything drew taut as the ropes attaching the sails to its mast. Aika caught Ariadne's eyes. She nodded once, a tiny gesture meant for her daughter alone.

Then she yelled, "Go, Minotaur!"

Aster swept Ariadne up in his arms and crossed the dock in several lengthy leaps. He kicked off, both feet shoving them upward and beyond the dock. Ariadne gasped as the ocean spread below them. She was helpless, held aloft by Aster, suspended between her past and future.

On the dock, Theseus and Aika approached Minos, and another person arrived.

Cadmun. What will become of them all?

She sensed it was the end for her father, and with his downfall, many things would change in Knossos. She was pleased to say farewell.

The wind stilled, the chasm beneath them yawned, seconds stretching impossibly as they arced through the sky. After what seemed like an eon, they landed on the boat with a teeth-clattering jolt.

The sailor stared at them, mouth agape. Somehow, fresh blood stained Aster's bandage. Her own arms were sore, her ribcage aching.

"I gripped you too hard," he said, breath making her freed curls dance.

"I'm fine. There is nothing to fret about." She hugged him, hiding her face in the fabric of his old shirt to suppress the sting of tears.

Embracing, they watched the dock, and its four current inhabitants, recede.

Chapter 10

Aster leaned on the side of the boat, moaning quietly. Ariadne massaged his back, letting her cool fingers linger on his neck. He ducked, tilting toward her, and mumbled his thanks.

"You've never sailed. This is normal, though regrettable." She tucked a wispy tendril behind his ear.

"And you?" He eyed her from the side, mouth quirking.

"I'm positive that my first boat ride occurred before I walked."

"Of course." His lids shuttered.

"It may seem impossible, but you will become accustomed to the sea," she said.

"Will we venture far?"

Ariadne leaned, her bare arm resting alongside his skin. "I cannot say. It depends... what happens with Minos."

Aster wiped his face with a sleeve. His pallor was more green than tanned, but he straightened to look at her.

"Will they overthrow him?"

"Yes," she said. "I saw the flash in my mother's eyes, as if she was finally awake." Ariadne paused, wishing she could share a more private exchange with Aika. "Cadmun will side with my mother, forming an alliance. Together, I can imagine they'll craft a convincing story for his dethroning."

"And how do you feel? Even after his cruelty, he remains your father." Aster wove circles on her forearm with his fingers.

She sighed. "It's only blood, nothing more. You're my family now."

Aster smiled softly, touching her neck.

Water sloshed the boat, carrying them westward. Eventually, Ariadne considered the sailor in charge of their vessel. The young man stood at the wheel, keeping his attention trained elsewhere.

"Sailor," she said.

He worried his lip. "Aye, your highness?"

"You are doing a fine job with this ship. What is your name?"

"Minnen, highness."

"Minnen. You obeyed King Minos promptly at the dock. Will you obey me, as the circumstances arise?"

"Aye, highness."

"Good. Thank you, Minnen. Do you know of an uninhabited place?

Somewhere we can exist, unbothered? It must be distant and secluded."

He appeared to debate his response, the inked designs on his muscled limbs shining with sweat. "Aye, I might, but there is no food on the island."

"We can fish," Ariadne said, glancing at Aster.

Minnen grimaced. "No fresh water, highness."

"We can catch the rain." She projected a certainty that rang false to her own ears.

"I have experience with that," Aster said.

Minnen swallowed, his focus sliding over Aster's formidable frame.

Ariadne threaded their fingers together. "I'm sorry. You probably would hate living like that again."

He brought their clasped hands to his lips, and she shivered at the pressure. "With you, I'll live anywhere."

"Truly?"

"Ariadne, I care only about being with you, whether we drink rain or seawater..."

She grinned, her nose wrinkling. "There's too much salt in seawater."

"Then I will learn all I need to."

"As will I. I've never lived outside a palace." Her admission roused a deep well of shame.

"And I've never lived in a palace. I think we will manage." Aster bobbed his head, resolute.

"It would seem we have a plan, then." She turned to Minnen, whose focus returned to sailing once more. "Minnen, you may have this ship once we arrive and I can assure you no harm will befall you. I hope the ship will be a fair reimbursement for your trouble."

"That is kind of you, highness," Minnen said, appearing unconvinced.

She squinted at the black streak of Crete. "Please, we must make haste. It is possible someone may come after us, though I doubt it will happen."

"Aye, princess."

Minnen adjusted the sails, scurrying here and there to increase their speed. Ariadne watched, transfixed by his skill. It was suitable for one person to manage, but he had to stay in motion.

"If you require assistance—"

He shook his head. "No, princess. Am fine. There is a room below, to get a break from the heat, if you need."

Ariadne blinked, taken aback by an inclusion of the lower deck.

"What did Minos intend for this vessel?" Aster asked.

"It was to take me and Theseus to his father's kingdom. It wouldn't be a long trip." Her voice trailed away. "I never intended to marry him."

Aster surrounded her, and she leaned her head on his chest.

"I wouldn't have begrudged you that."

"I was going to use him, as I was you, too."

The confession stung her more than him, it seemed.

He guided her so they stood facing each other. "I forgive you. Do you forgive me?"

"For what?"

"For lying," he said. "For claiming I didn't remember you, demanding you leave me…"

She relaxed. "I may not understand why you did that, but yes, you are forgiven."

"Good, thank you." He paused. "Do you want to venture below?"

"Oh." Her cheeks flamed, the heat radiating from her neck to her ankles.

Theseus and I would have been married in Knossos. Minos would have required it, which means this was to be our honeymoon vessel as well.

She glanced at Minnen, who assessed their surroundings with wide eyes, like throwing a net to sea and hoping to catch any form of explanation.

"No, I would rather see where we are going if you're comfortable."

"I am."

Aster stayed away from Minnen during their voyage, and Ariadne appreciated his consideration. Minnen had a food reserve, which he shared. King Minos had instructed him to finish painting the boat before the wedding. By Ariadne's estimation, he had succeeded, for the trails of color and designs looked pristine.

That evening, as Ariadne and Aster sat crossed legged on the bow, she untangled a thought.

"My father knew you weren't violent, but he argued you were a threat. How could I fail to fully see him, understand how despicable?"

"You weren't meant to," Aster said, tearing at a chunk of bread.

"The gods knew, too, and for making you suffer, I would destroy all of them if I could."

"Darling," he said, leaning close, his breath like wings on her skin.

"That's behind us now. Let us forget."

"You may forget, but I cannot. I wish I had come to you sooner." She ripped at her own bread.

His hands tangled in her hair, a desperation of the flesh. "It was soon enough."

They sat, rocking as the boat crested and sunk between waves. Neither spoke for some time. A few stars peaked out from the velvet evening sky.

"Minnen said we should be there before moonrise." She curled into the space between his arms.

"You're sure I am... what you want? This life we'll lead, just the two of us trying to survive. You're leaving everything, a life of comfort—"

Ariadne kissed him, lips fierce as a gale. They eddied as one, sharing breath and solace.

"Aster," Ariadne whispered. She thrilled at his resulting shiver. "I am leaving nothing and have found everything."

He squeezed her below the shoulders, swallowing. "I couldn't have imagined..." Aster tilted to the left, peering at her. "How can this be real?"

Ariadne ran her thumb over his chin. "I have no answer. And perhaps that's all right."

"And you do not mind my form? This wretched face?"

She brought her fingertips up, charting the ridge of his brow, the line of his jaw. "If you were wretched, would I choose to be this close to you?"

Moisture highlighted the range of color in his irises, greens and golds and browns.

"No, I suppose not."

She sobered. "You still do not believe."

"I don't know how to believe. I have never had reason to."

"Neither have I, not as I am." She pulled herself straight and took his hand. "And we've made a new path, filled with all the adoration we've lacked."

"Every bit of it." Aster traced the contour of her collarbone.

Propelled by an avid wind, the ship bounced over a wave.

"Shall we find a place to conquer?" Ariadne asked in jest.

"I'd rather not," he said with a partial grin.

"Oh, that's right. There will be no conquering."

His gaze softened. "Only contentment."

"And freedom. True freedom, the kind I never valued," she said.

He took in a great gulp of air, chest expanding against her. "Yes."

Nearby, Minnen changed the direction of the mainsail, humming a tune.

"I'm feeling less sick," Aster said.

"You're quite fast to adjust. Perhaps you'll be a sailor yet."

He peered at the horizon, and said, "I prefer the land, but there is a beauty to this."

She followed his gaze to the setting sun, only half of the orb visible over the shuddering horizon.

There is beauty in this, and we will make it ours.

Ariadne fell asleep with Aster under the spray of sea and stars. He laid her on a blanket, snatched from the bed below, and joined her. They slept deeply, two forms struck from the same raw, yearning matter.

Epilogue

Evening offered a melody of its own. Languid and subtle, each day sprawled into a welcome dusk.

They meandered amongst the trees, delicate plants tickling ankles. Their house rose in a clearing without walls. It was merely a roof standing aloft, and a floor packed firm. A vegetable garden inhabited the southern side. Minnen brought them seeds to cultivate, an unexpected and rare visitor they had embraced. He gave news of changes after Queen Aika assumed her dead husband's throne. They hadn't asked how the king met his end.

Since then, there had been no one else arriving on their shoe.

Waves sloshed upon the broken crags of the cove. Birds sleepily trilled as insects buzzed themselves into a humming frenzy.

A woman, no longer a princess, made her way to the water's edge.

A man, no longer a minotaur, paced behind her. They walked in single file, fingers twining like roots in the soil. Down the rocks they climbed, arms extended for balance. They left their clothes on an outcropping, piled without care.

The two entered the ocean, diving and resurfacing. Under the swelling revelation of stars, they touched once more.

"I love you, more than you'll ever know."

"You underestimate me." She wrinkled her nose. "I've always known you, haven't I?"

He chuckled, vibrant and billowing, and wobbled in the water. Even after some time, he wasn't the strongest swimmer, as if being unbound in the liquid bewildered him still. But he was improving. She swallowed her amusement at his temporary floundering, which he noticed. Unperturbed, he held her to him, hands spread against her back.

They traversed the light-sprinkled depths in unison, soaking in the saltwater of their home. Eventually, they would return to solid ground, but not yet. They lingered, buoyed and content, in a place both mortal and sublime.

Acknowledgments

Thank you to my dear partner and child who were tremendously patient and supportive during the crafting of this little book.

To all of my friends who helped make this possible: Chani Taylor, Zoë Gioja, Bridget O'Shaughnessy, Laurel Piety, Denise Brousard, and Dawn Adepoju, I appreciate all of you more than I can begin to express.

Chris Barcellona, my story editor, thank you, for helping heighten all I was going for with this tale!

About the Author

Briane Willis writes poetry, fiction, and non-fiction from her homestead in the Texas Hill Country. They dabble across genres and format.

Written in Leaves, a queer romance set in 1820s Paris, France, is their first novel. Their collection of short stories inspired by fairy tales and fantasy, entitled *A Mythology Woven,* explores darkness, hope, and healing. A duology of Greek mythology retellings, *By Your Eyes* and *Each Path a Red Thread,* investigate the burden of being called a monster, and the profound relief of acceptance.

Discover more at www.BrianeWillis.com.